MARK ENGLAND'S CAP

William Heinemann Ltd
Michelin House, 81 Fulham Road
London SW3 6RB

LONDON   MELBOURNE   AUCKLAND

First published 1990
Text © 1990 Michael Hardcastle
Illustrations © 1990 Margaret de Souza
ISBN 0 434 93065 2
Produced by Mandarin Offset
Printed in Hong Kong

A school pack of SUPERCHAMPS 7–12
is available from
Heinemann Educational Books
ISBN 0 435 00091 8

MARK ENGLAND'S CAP

MICHAEL HARDCASTLE

Illustrated by
MARGARET DE SOUZA

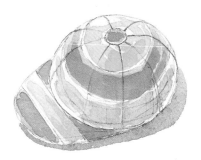

HEINEMANN · LONDON

Chapter 1

THE SUN WAS shining the first time Mark England put on his famous cap. In fact, the sun was just the excuse he'd been looking for; it was bright and strong and quite dazzling. Without a cap with a long peak a goalie would find it almost impossible to keep the sun out of his eyes when guarding the net at the Hawthorn Lane end of the pitch.

'Hey, where'd you get that dazzy cap, Mark?' Neil asked as soon as he saw it.

'A friend gave it to me, an old friend of my Grandad's, actually,' replied Mark, adjusting the angle of the peak to cut off the glare in the sky.

'Did he play baseball?' Ben wanted to

know. 'Looks just like a baseball player's cap to me.'

'It's not a baseball cap!' Mark replied indignantly. 'It's, well, it's a very special cap. That's why it's green-and-gold. Brazil's colours.'

'Doesn't even look like a football cap to me,' Ben pointed out. 'Are you sure it is one?'

'Must be!' Mark insisted. 'It probably belonged to a famous player. That's what my Grandad's friend says. He played lots of sports himself so he should know.'

'Oh yeah,' said Ben, losing interest. 'Well, I still think it looks like a baseball cap.'

Mark's team, Arun United, were playing a home match in the Under 12s Sunday League against Skerrington Swifts. It was an important fixture.

Skerrington, now in second place in the League table, were just two points ahead of United. So if United won today and gained three points they'd share top place in the League because Dowanhill, the leaders, weren't in action. Neil, Arun's captain and top goal scorer, had told them he expected 'maximum effort and total

concentration' from every player. That was his latest slogan, composed after listening to Football League managers being interviewed on radio sports programmes.

Neil won the toss and decided that Skerrington should have the sun in their eyes in the first half, which disappointed Mark who now wouldn't get the best use out of his cap for half-an-hour. The Swifts, however, attacked straight from the kick-off, determined to establish an early lead. In their black-and-yellow strip they buzzed at the opposition like the wasps they resembled; and Arun fell back to defend desperately.

Skerrington's tall, pacey striker fired in the first shot as soon as he had sight of the goal posts. Mark was distinctly lucky to keep it out of the net. His concentration was far from total because he'd been arranging his cap, pulling the peak down at this angle and then raising it at that angle. So he saw the ball only at the last moment. Flinging up an arm to protect his face he succeeded in deflecting the ball over the crossbar for a corner.

'You nearly gave 'em a goal there,' Neil muttered angrily as the Swifts prepared to take the kick.

'Rubbish!' Mark replied and leapt confidently to snatch the ball before an opponent could get in a header.

Soon Skerrington Swifts began to live up to their name with darting raids down the wings. A long cross from the right flank was aimed for the head of the leading striker. But Mark, judging his leap to perfection, came out to grab it in mid-air and then boot the ball well

upfield. Neil nodded his approval. That
was the sort of skill he expected from
his goalkeeper. Mark celebrated by
doing one of his handsprings on the
goal-line, the sort of comic act that
usually made his team-mates laugh.

A few minutes later, though, disaster
struck United.

This time the Swifts pushed forward
in strength, sending defenders up to
join the attack, along the left wing.

When the ball was lifted into the middle there were so many players around him that Mark had no option but to punch it clear. Unfortunately, the ball went no further than the back of Ben's neck. From there it rebounded downwards.

Mark knew he'd have to dive for the ball, smother it before an opponent could flick it into the net. As he flung himself forward into a forest of legs his shoulder collided with someone's knee, his head grazed a thigh – and his cap fell off. Horrified, he scrambled sideways to retrieve it before it could be trampled on by careless boots. The ball he had forgotten about bounced invitingly in front of an attacker. Gratefully he rammed it into the unguarded net for the important first goal of the match. The Swifts swarmed away in delight, mobbing the scorer as they went.

'You gave 'em that goal, absolutely *gave* it 'em on a plate,' Neil stormed at Mark.

'But somebody was going to stamp on my cap,' Mark pointed out.

'I wish they'd kicked your cap into the net instead of the ball,' Neil said unfeelingly. 'Look, take it off, Mark. You don't need it and –'

'But I do! The sun'll get in my eyes, so –'

'The sun's behind us! It should be bothering the Swifts this half, not you. That's why I chose the way we'd play instead of kicking off.'

That was hard to argue against. But Mark added quickly, 'Well, I'm getting used to it. I'm practising for the second half.'

Neil glared at him. 'Don't you let in another goal! Or else . . .' He stalked off to the centre for the re-start.

Mark was a bit jittery after that. Neil was not only the captain, he picked the team. Anyone who fell out with Neil wasn't likely to be chosen again for United. Mark's brother, Colin, was one of the subs for this match and he was a capable player. He could play in any position and would be delighted to be goalkeeper simply to get a game. So Mark knew he couldn't afford to make any more mistakes.

Soon the Swifts were flying towards him in another raid. When the ball reached Damon, the scorer of the first goal, he hit it perfectly. The ball, travelling like a bullet, went clean through Mark's hands and into the pit of his stomach. He doubled up, and his cap once again fell forward – this time, over his eyes.

Somehow Mark managed to clutch the ball but then he dropped it to shove the cap back. Damon, following up most efficiently, whoopingly slammed it into the net. *Arun United 0, The Swifts 2.*

Mark would have liked the ground to open up and swallow him. The goal really was his fault, though no one could have guessed that Damon possessed a shot as hot as that. Neil raced up and simply held out his hand for the cap. Silently, Mark gave it to him.

To his surprise, Neil sprinted to the touchline and passed the cap over to Colin, with a few accompanying words. Mark tried to signal to his brother to take good care of it but Colin took no notice. Mark thought he saw him stuff it into his sports bag. So it would get home safely, anyway. Mark's immediate worry was that Neil would replace him as goalkeeper but that didn't happen.

For the rest of the match he played brilliantly, even though the sun was in his eyes. Every shot that came his way he caught or punched out or tipped over the bar or round a post. Skerrington didn't score again and United snatched a draw through a fine solo goal by Neil and a last minute penalty kick.

'You see, you didn't need that stupid cap,' Neil told Mark as they left the field. 'You played terrifically without it. So don't wear it again for one of our matches, OK?'

'Mm,' Mark muttered, grumpily.

Chapter 2

By the time Mark reached home, there was no sign of Colin. 'He's gone to Sasha's for tea and then they're having a video party,' his mother explained. 'You can watch TV if you like till your tea's ready.'

But Mark couldn't concentrate on any of the programmes. His one thought was about his cap. So he was waiting to tackle his brother the moment he returned home.

'Come on, hand it over!' he ordered.

'Er, what do you mean?' Colin asked, unable to keep a look of guilt off his face.

'You know what I want. Hand that cap over or else. . . .'

'But you gave it to Neil, and he told me to get rid of it. Said it was ruining your game. So, well, I did. Sasha's Dad was collecting things to raise money for sick children in hospital. A good cause, he said it was. So that was why I gave him the cap. I mean, you did tell Mum the other day that you supported good causes when she gave your old sweater

away . . .' He trailed off, looking in dismay at Colin's horrified face.

'You did *what*?'

'Gave it to Sasha's Dad –'

'But it wasn't yours to give!'

'Neil said you didn't want it any more.'

'He couldn't have! I know he didn't want me to wear it any more, but – he couldn't just chuck it away!'

'He said, "He won't be wanting this any more. Do something with it." That's what he said.'

'You what!' Mark was staggered. He couldn't believe it. But he could tell Colin wasn't joking. 'I'll murder you if anything's happened to that cap. It's my – my most *valuable* possession. So, *where is it?*'

Colin gulped. 'It's in a sale to raise money for poorly children. It's called a charity auction and –'

'You can't do that to my cap!' exploded Mark. 'It wasn't your cap to give away, or Neil's. So get round there and get it back, sharpish.'

'No chance,' said Colin, very positively. 'You can't get things back that are in an auction, not unless you *pay* for them. That's a rule.'

'I don't have to pay to get my own cap back!' Mark yelled.

'It might fetch a lot of money,' Colin went on chirpily. 'Mr Fox, that's Sasha's dad, he said it was in good condition and a bit unusual. He said collectors are keen on that sort of thing now. He also said to tell you he was very grateful for your generosity. That's just what he said, Mark.'

For a moment Mark didn't know what to do or say. He was supposed to have a very quick brain: that's what Mr McKenzie, his teacher, had once told their class. Mark had spotted a way of solving a problem faster than anyone else. Mr McKenzie's praise meant a lot to him. Now he had to find a solution to an even tougher problem.

'When is this auction?' he asked.

'Next Saturday afternoon, I think,' replied Colin, confident now that his brother wouldn't attack him. 'Oh, and they're having a preview on Friday night. That's a chance for buyers to have a look at what's for sale.'

'I know what a preview is, I'm not ignorant and stupid like you,' Mark said fiercely. 'Will Mr Fox be there on Friday?'

'Expect so. I mean, he told me about it so he's sure to be. He'll want to see how keen people are to buy the best things in the auction. Then he'll know which ones will bring the top bids.' Colin paused, and started to smile. Mark recognised that look. It meant his brother was trying to be smart. 'Maybe your cap will make the most money of *everything*. Then everybody will say how *generous* you were to give it. You'll be a, well, a sort of hero, Mark!'

Mark didn't believe any of that. Well, perhaps some of it. His Grandad's friend had claimed that the cap really was special so perhaps it would fetch a big price. How was Mark going to afford to buy it? He went off to his room. Although he knew to a penny just how much he had in his savings account and his box with the secret lock, he counted it all up again. Hardly enough, he thought, to buy a priceless soccer cap at a charity auction.

He leaned on the ledge of the
window overlooking the common.
There had to be *some* way of making
money. But how? He watched a young
woman in a yellow tracksuit running
and throwing a ball as far as she could
for her dog to chase. Each time it shot
off like a rocket, bringing the ball back
for another throw. Both acted as if they

were in training for some athletics event. Mark didn't much care for dogs. They'd been known to attack while goalkeepers were actually making a save. Dogs were, dogs were – dogs were . . . *money!* Or could be.

For, suddenly, he remembered old Mrs Railton and her spaniel. A fat spaniel. A very fat spaniel, because he never got any exercise. Mrs Railton was too old to take him out herself.

'If ever you'd like a bit of pocket money I can give you a job,' she once told him. 'All you have to do to earn it, Mark, is to take Petkins out for a teeny-weeny walk.' Mark had never taken up that offer. But now . . . well, it would be one way of earning some money.

'Where are you going, Mark?' his mother asked as he dashed past her on the way to the front door.

'Taking a dog for a walk,' he called back.

'I don't believe this,' said Mrs England in a tone of wonder. 'You haven't got a dog – and you don't like going for walks.'

Sometimes, Mark told himself as he raced to Mrs Railton's, a boy doesn't have any choice in life. He heard Petkins long before the door was opened; and five minutes later the stout spaniel was still making protesting noises as Mark tried to persuade him to walk along Lovers' Lane. By the time Mark picked him up to get him home somehow, his arms were aching with the effort of dragging him along. The only thing that kept him from losing his temper was the thought of the money he was earning.

A week of tugging Petkins over the Common would just about finish them both off, Mark decided as he handed him back to his beaming owner. He was in despair – but Mrs Railton had some useful news.

'I've been thinking about what you told me,' she said. 'Well, I know that the Royal Hotel often has jobs for strong boys, the sort of jobs they couldn't pay a man to do full-time. Ask for Mr Talbot if you drop in there. He's always helpful, and he gives me the most divine doggy bags for Petkins whenever I go there.'

'Oh . . . er, right, thanks, Mrs Railton. I'll be round tomorrow, same time, to take Petkins for his walk.'

If he hadn't been so desperate for money that stuff about doggy bags would have put Mark off completely. But he was prepared now to try anything. Rather wearily he trudged back across the Common to try his luck at the old creeper-covered hotel where famous people sometimes stayed.

'Yes?' inquired the receptionist looking very suspiciously at Mark.

'Could I speak to Mr Talbot, please?'

'Well . . . I don't like to interrupt

him when he's busy. Was it important?'

'Yes, it is, really.' Mark was not going to be put off. He'd learned it was important not to give up when you desperately want something. It was the same determination that had got him his place as Arun United's goalkeeper.

Mr Talbot wore an apron and his sleeves were rolled up and he had a big, drooping moustache. But his blue eyes sparkled and he smiled warmly at Mark.

'Well, young sir, what can I do for you?' he asked, kindly. Mr Talbot, Mark decided instantly, was the nicest person he'd ever met. He would surely be ready to help him. So he explained who he was and why he was there; and he added that probably he was stronger than he looked and was willing to tackle anything.

'And how old are you, young Mark?'

'Nearly eleven.' Mark watched the old man nod thoughtfully.

'Well, I wasn't much older than you when I obtained my first employment in the hotel trade,' he said. 'I started as a boot boy. How would you like to do the same?'

Mark was puzzled. 'I'm sorry, sir, I don't know what that is,' he said with the same courteous manner that Mr Talbot displayed. The job didn't sound much fun.

'We like to look after our guests here as if they were in their own home,' Mr Talbot said. 'So we always clean their shoes for them if they'd like us to. At night they put them outside the bedroom door and I collect and clean them, returning them in time for them to be worn at breakfast. I have so many

jobs to do it would be a great help if
you could help with the boot-cleaning.
Does that appeal, young man?'

'Not much,' was what Mark wanted
to say. But he couldn't, not if he was to
earn money to buy back that cap. So he
replied: 'I'm keen to give it a go,
Mr Talbot.'

'Well done, young Mark,' said
Mr Talbot, giving his moustache an

upward brush with his forefinger. 'It'll mean an early start, though. *Very* early. Can you be here at six thirty? Earlier, if possible?'

Mark swallowed hard. He'd have to manage that somehow. So he promised to be there. They shook hands on it.

'Did you say it was a football cap you are anxious to buy?' Mr Talbot asked as they parted. Mark nodded. 'Ah,' said Mr Talbot, 'I prefer cricket myself. That's the game I used to play when I was your age. Very fond of cricket, I am. Still got all my cricket souvenirs. Well, I shall look forward to meeting you again tomorrow morning. Then you can tell me all about your sporting ambitions.'

Chapter 3

MARK'S WORRY THAT night was whether he would manage to wake early enough the following morning. His parents had finally agreed to his doing the jobs, since they knew where he'd be.

'But you'll have to get yourself up on time,' his Mum had added.

But he actually woke an hour before he had to and then his worry was that he'd drop off to sleep again. So he read a favourite football novel until it was time to creep down the stairs and make a quick breakfast. Mr Talbot had warned him not to start work on an empty stomach. 'First rule of working in the hotel trade – have a good breakfast before you start because you never know when you'll have the chance to eat again!'

There was a heavy mist over the Common as Mark crossed it. At the hotel Mr Talbot, waiting by an open door beside the stockroom, beamed at him.

'Well done, young man! I had every confidence you would be here on time. That's the mark of a good brain and a good worker. Oh, pardon me, no pun intended on your name!'

Mark laughed. He was quite used to people making jokes about his name. In his class there were two other Marks and because he himself was the middle one in age his teacher often called him Mark Two. Now they settled down in what Mr Talbot called the boot room, each of them with a hill of shoes in front of him.

'But how do we make sure they don't get mixed up, Mr Talbot? I mean, it would be awful if somebody got the wrong shoes back.'

'Ah, good thinking, that, Mark. That's why I always do this,' he explained, turning over the brown shoes he was holding to display a chalked number on the sole. 'That's the owner's room number. So he'll get his own shoes back all right.'

For a few minutes they didn't speak again because they were so busy applying polish and then making the leather gleam like a mirror. The job wasn't as bad as Mark had feared; he was quite enjoying working for Mr Talbot.

'Plenty of top football players have started life cleaning other players' boots,' Mr Talbot remarked as they sipped their mugs of tea during what he said was their interval for refreshments. 'It's a tradition for apprentices – new young players, you know – to clean the first team's dressing-room and their boots. That makes sure the youngsters don't get too big for their *own* boots! Oh, by the way, I've brought you a little gift.'

To Mark's astonishment he was handed a pair of gloves made of soft white leather. 'Those are inner gloves a wicketkeeper would wear inside his big gloves during a game. I've had 'em for years. Thought they might be useful to you, young Mark, when keeping goal.'

Mark was thrilled with the gift, and he wore the gloves as he ran home, money jingling in his pocket from his earnings. The gloves made him feel like a real professional and he was determined to live up to his name and play for his country one day as a goalie. Then he would have an England cap to add to the Brazilian cap – if, he reminded himself, he ever got it back from the auction.

He knew he was still a long way from having enough money to bid for it. Cleaning shoes and taking Petkins for walks was a slow way of earning. He might have to sell one of his

treasured possessions. Colin, he was
well aware, was desperately keen to
own Mark's pocket computer game.
How much, he wondered, would Colin
be prepared to pay for it?

'This isn't *your* normal lifestyle,' his
mother greeted him as he sat down for
a second breakfast, feeling he'd earned
it.

'Well, I've got to,' Mark said. 'I'm earning money to buy back my own cap that my rotten brother gave away.'

'Now that's enough, don't start on that again. Get on with your scrambled eggs,' Mrs England ordered, having had quite enough of her sons' arguments with each other.

That evening, after taking Petkins for another tug-of-war on the other side of the Common, Mark turned up for football practice. Neil believed that the team should get together as often as possible so that they always *played* like a team. This time he'd arranged a friendly match with Quadring Eagles, a team from a neighbouring village. Neil was a brilliant organiser as well as an inspiring captain. One day he was going to manage Scotland. he claimed. No one doubted it.

Colin arrived a few minutes after Mark, as usual: the brothers never did anything together, not even at home if they could avoid it. Now, to Mark's surprise, Neil told Colin he was being given a game in defence. 'Let's see how you get on in the back four,' the skipper said. 'We've got to be able to change our players about when we need to. Everybody's got to be versatile.' *Versatile* was the favourite word of the moment in football. Specialists were out and all-rounders were in. Neil always kept up with current fashions.

'Don't you score any own goals past me,' Mark warned his brother as they lined up for the start of the match. He frowned darkly as he said it.

'If you're any good as a goalie you won't let the ball go past you,' retorted

Colin. He'd decided that Mark wasn't going to do anything too violent to him after all for giving the cap away.

The Eagles were a better team than Neil had supposed. Like Skerrington Swifts, they attacked from the start like League champions, and United's defence wasn't really ready for them. Ben made the first blunder, allowing the ball to cannon off his knee so that it flashed just past Mark's left-hand post. Mark, remembering that Neil liked his players to talk to one another, told Ben off. Moments later Colin made a complete hash of a header and this time Mark just managed to catch the ball at the second attempt.

'I warned you, Colin!' Mark yelled. 'Do that again and I'll murder you!'

The Eagles, believing that United's defence was riddled with uncertainty and that their players even disliked one another, piled on the pressure. Mark became so nervous dealing with his own defenders' mistakes and Quadring's sharp-shooters that he let in a couple of shots he really ought to have saved. His luck was out, he felt, and he was sure it was because he'd lost his new cap.

'What's gone wrong with you?' Neil demanded at half-time. 'Not sulking, are you, because I told Colin to get rid of that silly hat?'

'Course not!' Mark protested. 'Our defence is playing like a bunch of onions. They just make you weep.'

'So are you,' Neil replied unsympathetically, and quite unfairly. 'If you make any more mistakes like the one that gave 'em their second goal I'm taking you off, Mark. I'll see if

Colin can do any better between the posts.'

'What!' Mark exploded. But by then Neil had moved off to have a word with one of his strikers. The captain knew that what he'd said would ensure that Mark played with total concentration in the second half. In his short experience of running a football team, Neil had learned some very useful tricks to get the best out of players.

That threat of being replaced by Colin did have its effect on Mark. He didn't let in another goal in spite of Quadring's determined attacks. Three times he displayed great bravery in diving headlong into dangerous situations to win the ball. After the first of the saves he tried out the white gloves Mr Talbot had given him, hoping that Neil wouldn't object when he noticed them (and there wasn't much Neil missed). They fitted amazingly well and Mark discovered he could handle the ball perfectly well in them. The gloves actually boosted his confidence.

'You see,' said Neil at the end of the match, which was a draw, 'you didn't need a silly hat to play like a hero in goal. Well done, Mark. See you next Sunday. Oh yes, and I like the gloves.

Make you look like a real pro.'

Mark glowed. Things were beginning to improve at last. He was back in favour as Arun United's goalkeeper; and he was beginning to earn some money; and he'd made a new friend in Mr Talbot. And Colin had actually apologised for what he'd done: he had tried to make amends by offering Mark three pounds for the auction from his own savings.

'You might need it,' he insisted when Mark rejected the offer. 'I wish you'd take it. I mean, I'll feel terrible if you don't get your cap back. Honestly, Mark, I didn't know it meant so much to you, otherwise I wouldn't have done what Neil said.'

'Well, all right, then,' Mark agreed, weighing his brother's coins in his hand. 'Tell you what: I know you've

always wanted my pocket computer
game. Well, I'll let you have it now –
for another two pounds. As long as you
pay now. Then I'll forgive you for
what you did.'

Colin swallowed hard. He really did
want that computer game but not at
that price, especially after he'd just
given Mark a contribution to the cap
fund. Still, he had the money and
Mark might never allow him a chance

of owning the game. Slowly, a little painfully, he counted out the money.

'Thanks,' Mark said, dropping the coins into his leather draw-string purse before handing over the black-and-gold game. 'Are you going to the preview of the auction tonight?'

'Er, don't think so. I want to watch a video with Gareth. It's about football training. You could come if you want to, Mark.'

'No thanks. More important things to do. I want to make sure they've still got my cap. And that I'll be able to get it back tomorrow.'

His mother remarked at tea that he was unusually quiet, which surprised Mark. He'd never supposed anyone would think he was noisy.

'Depends which way you look at things,' Mrs England pointed out. 'I mean, you're quiet enough when Colin isn't around. But when he's here you're always nagging him about something. No wonder the poor lad resents being a younger son. You really ought to be a bit kinder to him, Mark. After all, he is your brother.'

'But Colin's always saying stupid things about me, making up crazy jokes about my goalkeeping, stuff like that,' Mark protested. 'I get fed up with it.'

His mother smiled. 'That's only because he's *younger* than you. He never has the chance to be first at anything. Think about that, Mark, when you start to put him down next time. Will you do that?'

Mark turned a grimace into a sort of grin. 'I'll, er, do my best.'

Chapter 4

WHEN MARK REACHED the church hall
where the auction was to be held he
thought it must have started a day
early. There was hardly room to move
among the people milling around the
long trestle tables on which the items
were displayed. His hopes began to
sink. If so many people turned up to a
preview what chance had he of getting
the one thing he'd set his heart on?
Everything would be sold at terrific
prices. And a cap of such fame and
style would probably fetch a fortune.
Yet all Mark possessed was a few
pounds: a *very* few pounds.

It took him some time to find the
green-and-gold cap. Lying next to an

old cricket ball and a tennis racket with broken strings, it wasn't in the prominent position Mark felt it deserved. On the other hand, perhaps that would mean people would think it wasn't worth much. So they wouldn't make high bids for it. Mark's freckled face assumed a brighter appearance.

'Looking for a bargain, are you, young man?' a voice inquired somewhere behind his right ear.

'Er, I'd like that cap,' replied Mark, turning to look at a tall, grey-haired man with craggy eyebrows and a brightly-spotted bow tie.

'Would you now? Well, I expect it'll be a popular item, that one,' the man told him, nodding his head as if it were heavy with wisdom. 'Be some keen bidders for such a handsome cap. It's in excellent condition, too.'

45

Mark knew all that. 'It used to be *my* cap,' he started to explain. 'I mean, I think it still is, really. . . .'

But he gave up trying to explain when he saw how high the man's eyebrows had lifted. Plainly he didn't believe a word Mark was saying. Mark himself knew that his words had sounded unreal.

'Ah well, we'll have to see what happens tomorrow, won't we?' the man added. 'It's rather unusual to have someone trying to buy back his own, er, property. *Most* unusual.' Then he moved away, shaking his head in a rather sad manner.

Mark wanted to go after him to explain properly what had happened – but he supposed it wouldn't do any good. All that mattered was what took place at the auction itself. After glancing enviously at one or two interesting-looking books on football he left the hall.

There was a rank of shops at the end of the street where he lived and there he paused and sniffed the air. Ah, the smell of frying chips: surely there wasn't a better chip shop in the entire world than Jim's Takaway. Jim's slogan was 'If you've had your chips from here you'll never eat anywhere else!' Mark was one of Jim's devoted supporters. Nobody made better chips than Jim. But Mark mentally counted his money and decided that for once he'd have to deny himself a bag of the best. Tomorrow at the auction he might need every single penny he possessed. He trudged on home.

Chapter 5

THE NEXT MORNING, Mark was thankful to have jobs to do that kept him busy.

'We're off to the baths this afternoon, going to have some dead good races,' Colin said at lunchtime. 'Want to come?'

'You *know* I can't,' retorted Mark, annoyed. 'You know it's the auction.'

'Oh, yes, sorry, I'd forgotten. Well, I hope everything turns out OK.'

Then they shook hands, something they'd never done before except when their mother had ordered them to after a fierce quarrel.

Although Mark arrived at the church hall fifteen minutes before the doors were due to open there was already a

queue of bidders. Hastily he parked his
bike and then joined the queue just
ahead of another batch of arrivals.

'Keeping a place warm for somebody,
is that it?' asked the woman in front of
him.

'Sorry?' Mark hadn't a clue what she
was talking about.

'I mean, are you standing there in
place of somebody, your Dad, your

49

Mum, who's coming later? she went on, treating him like an idiot.

'Oh no,' Mark replied indignantly. 'I'm perfectly capable of acting for myself.' After that, she didn't speak to him again.

He thought that a lot of people looked as if they had plenty of money: and so they would be able to buy whatever they wanted. On top of that, as this was an auction for charity, people wouldn't mind spending a bit more than was necessary. 'It's all in a good cause, that's what they'll say,' Mark's mother had warned him. His gloom deepened; and his hopes fell further still when he saw the man with the craggy eyebrows hovering by the table on which the cap lay. He was certain the man would be his chief rival when bidding began.

The money that started to change hands astonished him. The auctioneer was somebody he hadn't seen before, a jolly, round-faced man with a very amusing style who seemed to know every bidder. Sometimes he could persuade a reluctant customer to go a little higher:

'Come on, Mr Andrews, you can afford to go up another pound if you cut out those chocolate bars every day!'

One or two children joined in the bidding, and the auctioneer simply dealt with their bids as with everyone else's. Mark was glad about that: he had been afraid that he might be barred from bidding because of his age or, even worse, be made fun of in front of everyone.

Then, to his surprise and delight, he spotted Mr Talbot, standing on the edge of the crowd and stroking his moustache. It was a while before Mark caught his eye. The old man nodded to Mark, and came over to join him.

'Are you going to buy something?' Mark whispered.

Mr Talbot gave a sort of shrug. 'Might do. I've got my eye on one or two cricket items it would be a pleasure to have. Depends what they fetch, though.'

'I think there's somebody else who's after my cap,' Mark told him. 'That man over there with eyebrows like diving boards. I think he's keen on it.'

'Oh yes,' was all Mr Talbot said. He didn't appear very interested.

Mark became impatient. The auctioneer was taking a long time to get to the goods on the cap table; and even then he seemed to spend an age selling old photographs of cricketers, a shoe worn by a famous racehorse, a golf umbrella and a signed football. Mr Talbot bid for the photos and a battered cricket bag but didn't get them. Mark was too excited to say anything about his new friend's disappointment.

'And now,' declared the auctioneer, picking up the prized cap, 'we have here an object that's attracted a lot of interest. Some think it's a famous international footballer's headgear, others believe it once adorned the head of a leading cricketer. I'm not going to tell you *who* it belonged to because I never saw the original owner wearing it. And you know I never tell a lie – well, not in front of all you honest people!'

There was a little laughter at that,

but Mark didn't join in. He just wished
the man would get on with the selling.
His right hand was ready to shoot high
to signal his bid, while his left clutched
the bag of money in his pocket.

'So, what am I bid for this colourful
cap, this handsome headgear, this –'

'One pound – no, two pounds!' Mark
sang out.

That caused a laugh in the hall.

'Steady on,' murmured Mr Talbot.

'Don't overdo it.'

'Now that's what I call a keen bidder,' remarked the auctioneer. 'He raises his own offer before anyone else can say a word!'

One person who was neither laughing nor looking at Mark was the man with eyebrows like balconies and spotted bow-tie. He was telling the auctioneer of his higher bid.

'Ah-ha,' rejoiced the auctioneer, 'I scent a battle in prospect.'

And that's what it became. It was a battle between just the two of them, Mark and Mr Eyebrows, going up steadily, by one pound at a time. Mark raised his hand immediately, whereas his opponent did not put in his own bid until both Mark and the auctioneer thought he'd given up the fight.

'It's just his tactic to focus attention on himself,' Mr Talbot whispered.

Mark nodded sadly. He sensed that his opponent could go much higher than his own sixteen pounds. He had just bid fourteen, and his mouth was dry.

'Sixteen,' said the Eyebrows, raising the total two pounds suddenly.

Mark gulped. That was it. He knew that everyone was looking at him, waiting for his reply; but he kept his hand in his pocket. 'I haven't any more money,' he said to Mr Talbot out of the side of his mouth. His friend nodded – and then raised a finger to put in his own bid!

'I don't want *you* to buy it for me,' Mark said hurriedly. 'I –'

'I'm bidding for myself,' Mr Talbot said softly. 'I told you I collect cricket souvenirs.'

'Oh, sorry.' Mark felt abashed. So he wasn't going to get the cap after all. All his planning had come to nothing.

But then he suddenly realised what Mr Talbot had said. So it must be a *cricket* cap after all – not the soccer cap he'd thought it was! Mr Talbot knew about this sort of thing. Maybe Grandad's friend had been mistaken – or just joking about Brazil. Mark's disappointment began to melt away. He hadn't suffered such a terrible loss after all.

To the crowd's obvious delight, the struggle for the ownership of the colourful cap continued for a few more moments. Then, with a sigh of resignation, Mr Talbot gave in. 'Thirty pounds is too much for me,' he said as Mr Eyebrows raised the total yet again.

'Gone! Sold to the gentleman over here for twenty-eight pounds,' declared the auctioneer.

'I'm sorry you didn't get it, Mr Talbot,' Mark told him. 'Really sorry.'

'Oh well, some you win, some you lose,' said his friend with a shrug and a little whisk of his moustache. 'Anyway, I've got –'

But before he could say what he'd

got they were interrupted by
Mr Eyebrows, now clutching the cap
he'd bought at such high cost.

'Sorry you fellows lost,' he said
gruffly, looking from one to the other
of them. 'But you see, I had to have
this cap. Means everything to me. It's
the cricket cap of my old college.
Opened the bowling for them in my
day, I did. Then, like a fool, I lost *my*
cap when we moved house. Never had
a chance of getting another until this
auction came up. Was amazed to see it
here. Happiest days of my life were at
that college, playing cricket.'

'Then I'm glad you got it,' Mr Talbot
told him. 'Memories are everything at
our age.'

The new owner of the cap nodded his
thanks and then drifted away.

'Think I'd better be getting home,

too,' announced Mark. 'Nothing to stay for now, is there?'

'Not really,' agreed Mr Talbot. 'But, Mark, I don't want you to go away empty-handed. I think you deserve a reward for all your determination. Oh, and your planning. I admire that. So I've bought this for you. I think it'll fit because you're not the big-headed sort!'

From an inside pocket he drew out a large envelope containing a red-and-white cap.

Mark gasped. 'But those are the colours of my favourite team,' he exclaimed.

Mr Talbot smiled. 'I remembered your telling me – and this is a real goalkeeper's cap. Try it on, Mark.'

It fitted as if it had been made just for him. Although there wasn't a mirror to look into Mark knew it would look just right.

'But why did –' he started to ask, when Mr Talbot interrupted.

'You didn't know the cap in the auction was for cricket but I suspected it was. I also knew that it wasn't right for you even if you had managed to buy it. A footballer like you should

wear a footballer's cap. That's why I got it for you.'

'But you shouldn't –' Mark began, when Mr Talbot held up a hand.

'Look, I've enjoyed your company these past few mornings, Mark. This is my way of saying thank you for your company and your help. An old man like me can please himself what he does with his money. Just like the chap who bought the green-and-gold cap. Anyway, I hope it brings you luck wherever you play.'

'Oh, I'm sure it will,' replied Mark, tugging down the peak. 'It feels terrific already. I can't wait to keep goal in it.'

Mr Talbot gave his moustache an extra tweak. 'That's the spirit,' he said with a grin.

Helen Cresswell
ROSIE AND THE
BOREDOM EATER
0 434 93061 X

Gwen Grant
THE WALLOPING
STICK WAR
0 434 93055 5

Carmen Harris
NAOMI'S SECRET
0 434 93107 1

Mary Hoffman
DOG POWDER
0 434 93059 8

Robert Leeson
HOW ALICE SAVED
CAPTAIN MIRACLE
0 434 93063 6

William Mayne
THE MEN OF
THE HOUSE
0 434 93085 7

Sam McBratney
THE THURSDAY
CREATURE
0 434 93089 X